SO-ARG-022

Cheddar's Tales

SHOWDOWN
in Crittertown

By Justine Fontes
Interior illustrations by Ron Fontes

Happy Thoughts!
Justine

BARRON'S

Dedication

For my father, Marvin Korman,
who shared his love of cheese,
books, music, and art.

Copyright © 2014 by Justine Fontes

Cover illustrations by David Mar
Interior illustrations by Ron Fontes

All rights reserved.
No part of this publication may be reproduced or distributed in any form
or by any means without the written permission of the copyright owner.

All inquiries should be addressed to:
Barron's Educational Series, Inc.
250 Wireless Boulevard
Hauppauge, NY 11788
www.barronseduc.com

ISBN: 978-1-4380-0360-3

Library of Congress Control Number: 2014931541

Date of Manufacture: April 2014
Manufactured by: B12V12G, Berryville, VA

Printed in the United States of America
9 8 7 6 5 4 3 2 1

Introduction

Dear Children,

Have you read my first book yet? If you haven't, here's what you need to know: My name is Cheddar. But folks around here call me the Postmouseter, because I am the first leader of the Critter Post—a group of animals dedicated to spreading happy thoughts.

We got the idea from the human post office. My colony lives in the basement of the post office in Crittertown, Maine. We started getting lots of ideas after "The Change," when animals suddenly understood human speech and writing. Critters can talk to each other, but people still only hear squeaks, barks, and chirps. We get around that problem by writing letters.

When we found out that the Crittertown

Post Office might close, my friends Grayson, Nilla, and I went on a mission to find a new home. We met mean mice at the store next door, and some very smart mice at the library. And by writing notes, we made friends with the third graders at Crittertown Elementary School. They helped us save the post office!

If you want to know more, please read *Cheddar's Tales: Crisis in Crittertown*. Otherwise, just turn the page and think…

…happy thoughts!

Cheddar Plainmouse
The Postmouseter

P.S. If you have questions or just like to write letters, you can reach me at:

Cheddar Plainmouse
1138 Main Street
Crittertown, ME 04355

Chapter 1 *Not Again!*

Most mice hate humans. But the way I see it, the critters who invented cheese can't be all bad.

Besides, these days some of my best friends are humans—the small humans of Mrs. Olson's third grade class at Crittertown Elementary School. These kids helped save our home! So we started "hanging out" together every weekday after school. Human expressions are so strange. Hanging out has nothing to do with hangers or clotheslines. But it is fun!

I like hanging out at the post office with my mouse friends Grayson and Nilla. You never know what you're going to find in the trash cans, in the recycling bins, and on the snack table. Once we found half a hamburger!

In late November the treats really piled up. We sampled homemade fudge, Christmas cookies, nuts, and a "cheese log." That's not as weird as it sounds. Forget trees; this was soft cheese pressed into the shape of a log. And like every other kind of cheese, it's so delicious!

Anyway, one night after closing time, we went upstairs for some treasure hunting. But we found something that made our fur stand on end.

Grayson suddenly squeaked, "Closing the school!"

Nilla dropped the muffin wrapper she'd been nibbling. "What?"

I raced up the Priority Mail display to join Grayson at the community bulletin board. As the grandson of our colony's leader, Grayson had an interest in politics. He often read the notices about town council meetings. Usually they just talked about the cost of snowplows and other things that didn't matter to us. But this…

I read the words twice and then moaned. "They can't do it!"

Nilla reads more slowly than I do. So she asked, "Who can't do what?"

Grayson answered, "The council is going to discuss closing Crittertown Elementary School!"

Nilla squeaked with joy. "No more homework, no more math, and we could play with the children all day—not just in the afternoons! Why do you look so glum?"

Grayson shook his head. "The kids would still have to go to school. They just wouldn't go right here in town."

I read to the end of the notice. "The plan is to merge with Lakeville Elementary, which is a larger, newer school about 20 miles from here."

Nilla looked as sad as the time we opened the clerk's cookie tin and found a sewing kit instead of shortbread. I hated to explain the worst part. "Our friends would have to take a bus to school. They'd be gone longer each day. And we might lose the playground."

Nilla wailed, "I love the playground!"

I shrugged. "Well it's one of the things that needs costly repairs."

We felt almost too low to check the snack table. But we knew the rest of the colony was

counting on us. So we each grabbed a cookie
to slide under the worn rubber seal on the post
office's back door.

As soon as we entered the basement, our
cookie-loving comrades swarmed.

Someone squeaked, "Did you get any of the
ones with sprinkles?"

"I like icing!"

"Any brownies?"

Only our nervous friend, Twitchy, sensed something was wrong. Of course, Twitchy always thinks something is wrong. Sadly, sometimes he's right!

Twitchy asked questions in a frightened rush. "What is it? Have the postal bosses changed their minds? Will they be closing the office after all?"

Grayson shook his head. "The elementary school."

Twitchy sighed with relief. "That's okay. As long as we have a home."

Twitchy was a real stay-in-the-nest type of mouse. He hadn't gotten to know the children yet. He couldn't understand why this news made us so gloomy.

Our leader, Brownback, understood. He said, "It's not good for the town—not to

mention your young friends." Then he sighed.
"But what can we do about it?"

I thought about writing a letter to the
children. But I felt too depressed. I tried
cheering myself up by thinking of different
cheeses in alphabetical order, from American
to blue all the way to Stilton. (If you know any
cheeses that start with T, U, V, W, X, Y, or Z,
please let me know!)

All that did was make me hungry. So instead
of cheese, I tried thinking of ways to save the
school. I figured that since letters helped save
Crittertown's post office, maybe they could save
the school, too.

I started a list of humans to whom we might
write. I hoped the children could add to it the
next day. We always met at April's house,

because she lived next door to the school. Her garage was empty all day while her father was at work. April's mom worked at home, typing on a computer and talking on the phone. So we didn't have to fear someone shrieking "Mouse!" and calling an exterminator.

That afternoon, Buttercup came to pick us up as usual. His human friends, Jill and Bill, always came to April's house. And Buttercup— the large, yellow Lab—never missed a chance to spend time with his favorite people. Buttercup lived at the Bed & Breakfast. But he had the run of the town, as long as he came home in time for supper. With his love of food, that was never a problem.

As soon as the big dog arrived at our hole, Grayson, Nilla, and I rushed out to greet him.

Buttercup lowered himself to the scraggly grass so we could climb onto his back.

For a dog who "barely knows rollover from beg," Buttercup was quite alert. As we settled onto the soft scruff under his collar, he sensed something was wrong.

"What're you worrying about?" he barked. "You can tell me. Did someone get stuck in a trap? Did those mean mice from the store try to invade the post office? Did Mike's wife put him on another diet?"

"Nothing like that," Grayson said.

"Then what is it?" Buttercup stood up and started walking.

Nilla exclaimed, "The school! The grownups are planning to close Crittertown Elementary School!"

Buttercup nodded. "Now it all makes sense!"

"What makes sense?" I asked.

Buttercup stopped to scratch his ear. We struggled to cling to the back of his neck. "Sorry," he muttered. "I always scratch when I'm thinking."

Buttercup resumed walking and talking. "I was trying to recall what I'd heard Jill and Bill say this morning when they brought my food."

Grayson muttered, "Probably couldn't hear over his own gulping."

Buttercup laughed. "No, I heard them. I just didn't know what it meant. They said something about having to take a bus instead of walking to school if 'the budget crisis' didn't get resolved. What's a budget crisis?"

I sighed. "Humans arguing about money."

The library mouse named Economics knew all about this sort of thing. I only knew that humans often worried about money, and this definitely interfered with the flow of happy thoughts.

When we reached the garage, the children were talking about the same thing. There wasn't enough money to fix Crittertown Elementary School, so the Crittertown kids would have to attend Lakeville. Jill said, "Taking a bus means leaving earlier and coming home later, and we might be not able to meet here as often!"

Ian said, "I've heard Lakeville has a good music room. But it won't be the same."

Tanya jumped up. "Then let's not let it happen!"

"What can we do?" her friend Hannah asked.

11

I held up my list. Jane read it out loud. "Humans we could write letters to about saving Crittertown Elementary School: politicians, parents, media."

Wyatt said, "Great idea! Our letters helped save the post office."

"We can write petitions, too," April said in her sweet whisper.

When everyone asked, "What?" Javier repeated, "Petitions."

"Yes!" Tanya exclaimed. "Let's start tomorrow!"

Andy said, "Maybe other classes can help, too. We're not the only ones who want to save our school."

"Good thinking!" Wyatt agreed.

So we wrote a letter and a petition. Until Bill

said, "This is too much like schoolwork. Last one to the playground is a rotten egg!" Then he took off running.

Jane scooped up Grayson, Nilla, and me into her hat and ran to the schoolyard. We bounced around wildly until she reached the swings.

Nilla was still puzzling over what rotten eggs had to do with running when Jane started swinging. Then we all forgot about everything, shouting, "This is fun!"

Chapter 2 *Mess-Up at the Meeting*

Mrs. Olson liked the idea of the letters and a petition. She sent Andy to Principal Clark's office to ask about involving the other classes.

Tanya said, "Maybe the junior high and high school kids can help, too!"

Mrs. Olson smiled. "Please raise your hand, Tanya. But yes, that's a good idea. After all, lots of those students graduated from here."

Before the school day was over, teachers and students all over Crittertown were behind the campaign. We heard this from Chitchat, one of the red squirrels who lived near the school.

Grayson thought he was "an awful gossip." But I didn't mind the squirrel's chatter. Chitchat always knew what was going on, and he'd become a very useful member of the Critter Post. I could always count on him to carry a message. After all, gossip is all about carrying messages!

"They'll talk about the letters and petitions at the meeting tonight," Chitchat reported. "I heard that straight from the school secretary."

"We should go to that town council meeting, too!" Grayson squeaked.

I shuddered at the thought of all those humans and cars gathered at the school. We hadn't set one paw inside Crittertown Elementary since Principal Clark called the exterminator and destroyed our dream of living there.

Grayson went on. "It's the only way to find out what we're really up against."

I said, "You're just curious about human government—and you're always looking for any chance to get out of the basement."

Grayson grinned. "You know me so well."

Nilla squeaked, "Learning all we can will help us solve the problem."

I sighed. Two against one meant I would not be spending a nice, quiet evening under the post office.

Buttercup agreed to be our taxi to and from the meeting. As usual, Brownback wanted us to keep him informed. So I wore out my paw taking notes.

The grown-ups argued over which repairs were really necessary. They argued over whether it would be better to build a new school. And they argued over whose turn it was to talk.

Just when I thought I couldn't stand any more, the grown-ups stopped for "refreshments."

Nilla nudged me, "That's food, right?"

I nodded. Food might mean… Many busy hands lifted the lids off plastic containers and pulled back shiny plastic wrap. Suddenly the room filled with that most delicious smell: cheese!

Nilla grabbed my tail just in time. I almost rushed out among all those people!

I whispered, "Thanks."

We watched humans consume cookies and cheese. "Drop crumbs!" I urged silently. But they usually chomped the pieces of cheese in one big bite.

Leave leftovers! I thought. But I feared they would eat the whole feast right down to the paper doilies.

Slowly, oh so slowly, the meeting started breaking up. People drifted into the lobby. Some said their good-byes. Others continued talk-talk-talking.

Suddenly, the voices grew louder. Grayson's eyes gleamed with excitement. "It's a fight! I wonder if they're going to bite or scratch each other."

Nilla squeaked, "Let's go see!"

But I had a different idea. While all attention focused on the fight, I ran to the cheese! I grabbed a huge wedge of my favorite— cheddar! It was nearly as big as me. But I had it perfectly balanced on my back. Then I

suddenly heard someone scream!

"What's wrong?" I wondered.

Then the screamer added, "A mouse!"

Other voices chimed in, including Principal Clark. "I told that exterminator this place was infested. But he said he saw no sign of vermin."

Vermin—that word really hurt! But I had no time to feel insulted. With deep regret, I dropped the cheese and raced into the night.

I found Grayson and Nilla under Chitchat's maple tree. We heard the grown-ups talking as they walked to the parking lot. The debate was over.

This was "proof" that the old building was "infested with vermin." The school would be closed!

My heart sank. It was my fault! If only I'd waited until the people were gone. They might have dropped some cheese. They might have thrown some away. People were always throwing away great treasures. But no, I'd let my stomach do the thinking instead of my brain. And now…

Nilla tried to console me, "It's not your fault. It's the numbers. You heard Principal Clark. The budget and the bills just don't add up."

Ever since our time at the school, Nilla had been studying math. Of course, she still had a long way to go. Nilla said, "I don't understand why they can't borrow some ones from somewhere or move some decimal points or something. In any case, Cheddar, there's no sense blaming yourself."

That was sweet of her to say, but I did blame my greedy love of tangy, savory cheese. Maybe I really was vermin!

Thanks to me, the children would be traveling 20 miles to school. Buttercup couldn't possibly carry us all the way to Lakeville Elementary School. My misery deepened as I realized what it all meant. No more story time! No more listening through the windows while Mrs. Olson read out loud.

I moaned, "There must be something else we can do to save the school!" But I couldn't think of anything. I groaned. "I wish I were smarter." Then I realized, "I don't have to be smarter. I just need to squeak to someone who is!"

"That's easy. Everyone's smarter than you mice—except Buttercup," teased a voice from above.

Chitchat climbed toward us headfirst from the maple's top branches. The squirrel chattered on, "Do you need me to get that goofy dog, or should we wait until all the cars are gone?"

Grayson surveyed the emptying parking lot. "It won't be long. We might as well wait." He added, "Besides, I want to know what Cheddar's talking about."

I said, "Let's ask Buttercup to take us to the

library. We can ask our friends for ideas."

Nilla asked, "Which subjects?"

All the library colony mice were named for different book categories.

Grayson sighed. "Economics, I suppose."

Economics thought the world revolved around money. He was so boring!

I knew which subject Grayson would rather visit. I felt the same way. But I teased him anyway. "I know you'd rather squeak to Poetry."

Nilla mused, "Economics is money, like budgets and bills, right?"

"Exactly!" I squeaked. "Maybe Economics or Nonfiction will know how to save the school." Nonfiction was the library clan's leader.

"It's worth a try," Grayson agreed. Then

he smoothed his fur, and I knew what he was thinking. As long as we were at the library, we'd see Poetry!

Chitchat said, "I can take that message to Buttercup. And I'll let your colony know you'll be getting back to the post office later than expected."

"That's wicked decent of you," I said. "Thanks a lot, Chitchat!"

The squirrel hurried away. His bushy tail soon disappeared between the bare twigs. The cold, quiet night surrounded us. Stars twinkled in the big, black sky. The moon looked like a pale sliver of cheese. But, for once, I didn't want to think about cheese.

A few dim lights shone on the school. I shuddered. Would the humans really close it?

What if the kids started staying after school in Lakeville? Would they forget about us and the Critter Post?

Buttercup's bark stopped my brooding. "All aboard for the library!" he said, adding, "It's about time I gave Dot a good teasing."

"She deserves it!" Nilla agreed.

Nilla had never gotten over our brief contact with the library's cat. The library colony was used to Dot's evening friskies, but we had never seen a cat close-up before. Those huge claws, sharp fangs, awful pounces, and the mocking laughter of her hunting chatter still haunted our nightmares.

Buttercup laughed. "I like to see Dot's tail fuzz up when I bark."

I shuddered. Everything about that cat

terrified me, especially her eyes. It was nice to think our dog pal was big enough to tease Dot.

We clung to Buttercup's collar as he trotted from the school to the library. We usually made this journey during the day to be with the children. In the dark everything seemed different.

The streets were so quiet! No cars, no dog walkers—just the soft pad of Buttercup's paws. Then he paused to sniff the air.

"We're not alone," he barked softly.

"No you aren't, house dog!" howled a coyote emerging from behind a bush.

"Looky here!" another coyote bayed.

Other howls answered those. Grayson, Nilla, and I strained our eyes trying to spot the whole pack. My friends pressed closer to me, and we all tightened our grip on Buttercup's collar.

"Why are you carrying those snacks on your back?" the lead coyote asked.

"They're not snacks," Buttercup growled. "These are very important mice. They are the three who saved the post office."

The coyotes laughed cruelly. "What's the post office?" one howled.

"Who cares?" the leader replied as his pack circled Buttercup.

"Can you eat it?" another wondered.

I had never been so near a coyote before. From a distance, they looked like skinny dogs with scraggly fur. As they came closer, the coyotes seemed more like tall foxes than dogs. Or maybe that was just the cold menace in their eyes.

Buttercup opened his big mouth and barked as loud as he could. "Bow wow wow, woof, woof, WOOF!"

Dogs in nearby houses started barking, too. Lights turned on. Human voices asked things like, "What is it, boy?" and "Something out there?"

The coyote leader howled, "Let's go!" and his pack mates howled their answers. They knew a barking dog would bring humans with guns. So off they loped.

Nilla exhaled. "Whew! That was scary!"

Suddenly realizing I'd been holding my breath, I exhaled too.

Grayson bragged, "Buttercup could've taken them! He just didn't want to get in trouble, right, Buttercup?"

The Lab said, "Not smart to take on a whole pack. One coyote, sure, but they rarely travel alone."

"You did the right thing." I patted one of his soft ears. "The Critter Post can't afford to lose you. And if you got hurt, you'd have to go to the vet."

Buttercup hated the animal doctor as much as he despised skunks. He chuckled to himself, recalling, "The last time I was at the vet's I teased a cat. You should've seen how fat her tail fuzzed when I barked!"

Nilla stared into the dark night and said, "Let's not talk about cats, okay?"

"Okay," Buttercup agreed. Then he stopped suddenly.

Grayson asked, "What is it?"

Buttercup tilted his head, listening. Then we heard it, too. A rustling, rattling sound near some garbage cans in front of the next house.

Nilla grabbed one of my paws and squeezed it hard. I knew what she was thinking. Stray cats like garbage cans.

I opened my mouth to remind her that Buttercup could protect us. But the dog spoke first. "Raccoon," he said, just as the black-masked critter trotted into view.

The raccoon kept his distance as his bright eyes stared at us with amusement. "Why carry someone on your back?"

Buttercup said, "These mice are my friends."

The raccoon laughed. "My friend is any garbage can with a loose lid, or an apple tree that's heavy with fruit." Then he waddled away, chuckling to himself. "Stupid dog! Wouldn't catch me carrying anything but my own supper."

My body sagged with sadness.

Nilla felt my shoulders droop. "What's wrong?"

I sighed. "Not every critter has Critter Post potential. Some don't get the idea of working together or caring about anything beyond themselves."

Grayson said, "We don't need a bunch of flea-bitten raccoons or trashy street gangs with fangs."

Buttercup agreed. "Even cats have more Critter Post potential than coyotes."

Nilla shuddered. "Let's stick to squirrels, chipmunks, dogs, and birds."

Buttercup took a few steps and then froze again. We didn't have time to ask why. We didn't need to. Six deer leaped off the nearest yard onto the pavement.

Ever seen a deer up close? They're big, tawny animals with long, skinny legs and dark, wide eyes. Why are they so beautiful? You just want to stare at them and wish they would stay, like a rainbow.

That night we weren't the only ones staring. The deer stared at us and Buttercup. They made soft sounds among themselves. I saw the

traces of spots on the smallest four. I figured they must be fawns, and the other two their mothers.

The largest doe spoke. "Are you the noisy dog named Buttercup?"

"Yes," the Lab replied in a gentle whisper, trying not to spook them.

The doe went on. "Are these the mice who saved the post office?"

Grayson stood up and bowed. "We are."

Both does bowed gracefully. The fawns fumbled to imitate their mothers.

The doe said, "We are grateful. We don't like all people, but some feed us, some grow apples. Some bring a swift death to the weary. And the cleared roads make winter travel easier. So we are glad when this town prospers."

The deer bounded off as suddenly as they appeared, flashing their white tails. I thought, "No wonder Santa Claus uses deer to pull his sleigh. What could be more magical?"

Nilla felt the same way, because she squeaked, "That was… cheesetastic!"

I gasped. "I had no idea that even the deer had heard of us."

Nilla teased me, "You're famous now, Mr. Postmouseter."

Fame meant nothing to me. But the enchanted encounter gave me hope for our cause.

Chapter 3 *Putting the Fun in Fundraising*

As Buttercup trotted across the library's parking lot, we heard chattering in the trees. Chitchat was telling Rusty about the town council meeting.

The grumpy red squirrel groused, "I don't give a pinecone whether Crittertown has its own elementary school or not!"

Grayson chuckled. "Rusty only cares about his precious acorns."

A voice came out of the darkness. "That's because he's an old fool."

General History and two of his scouts stood between Buttercup and the entrance to the library's basement. General History went on. "The school has strategic value for humans and critters alike."

"What's strategic?" Nilla asked.

General History replied, "*Strategy* is planning for wars and other things."

"Oh." I could tell Nilla was about to ask another question. But General History went on. "I'm sure my grandfather will want to talk with you." A smile flickered across his serious face. "And my sister will be glad to see you, too."

As Buttercup lowered himself to the pavement, Grayson and I smoothed our fur. Grayson squeaked, "Cheddar, you can tell Nonfiction about the meeting while I visit Poetry."

I squeaked, "You can read my notes as well as I can."

Nilla sighed. "Fight over Miss Pretty Paws later. We have a school to save!"

Meanwhile, Buttercup sneaked up to the library's front window.

"What's he doing?" I wondered.

Grayson said, "Let's find out!"

We scurried up the drainpipe to peep in the window. Dot napped on the checkout desk. The orange and black spots on her white fur rose and fell with each breath. At least her horrible amber eyes were safely closed.

Buttercup took a deep breath. We all knew what that meant. Nilla tapped his paw and begged, "Please don't wake her! I can't go inside if that nightmare is awake."

The big dog let out his breath slowly and then sighed. "I guess I can wait until after you leave."

"Could you?" Nilla scrambled up his paw to kiss Buttercup's ear. "You're the best dog in the world!"

Buttercup wagged his tail so hard that his butt wagged, too, and we all laughed.

"I'll be back to pick you up—and scare the fuzz into Dot's tail—when the moon is high," the dog promised.

Then we followed General History and his scouts into the library basement.

As soon as we cleared the narrow passage, we all noticed the change.

Nilla whispered, "It's so crowded!"

I stared at a sea of eager eyes and twitching whiskers. I recognized lots of the library colony mice. But there were also many new faces among those squeaking, "It's them!" "It's the three!" "That's the Postmouseter!"

Several young mice stepped forward to introduce themselves. One squeaked loudly and clearly, "I'm Public Speaking. I work with Self Help."

The others also had "subtopic" names, like "Quilts," who was part of the Hobbies group; "International Cookbooks;" and "Computer Games."

I spotted Poetry near Nonfiction, her grandfather. She waved. But since Grayson stood next to me, I couldn't be sure if her smile was meant for him or me.

Nonfiction asked, "What did you learn at
the meeting?"

I handed him my notes. The old mouse read
them quickly. "Very thorough." Then he added,
"Neat paw-writing."

I blushed at the compliment.

Nonfiction went on. "Is it certain the school
will be closed?"

My blush deepened. Before I could describe
my ill-fated cheese run, Grayson said, "It

seemed so by the time the people left."

Nonfiction nodded. "Well, minds can be changed. Ways can be found."

Economics squeaked, "Fundraising is a popular topic."

Nilla nudged me. I shrugged.

Dictionaries explained, "Raising funds is gathering money for a charity or a cause."

Nilla squeaked, "That's what we need to do!"

The old mouse known as Local History spoke slowly. "Crittertown has hosted many fundraisers. The library, the Historical Society, the Fire Department…"

Nilla interrupted. "That's great. How do they do it?"

Local History droned on. "The library sells

used books. The Historical Society has 'wine and cheese socials,' inviting wealthy citizens to donate money. The Fire Department holds bean suppers, bake sales, and crafts fairs."

At the phrase *cheese socials*, my mind wandered to a pretty paradise where giant cheese wedges introduced themselves. "Hello, my name is Gorgonzola, and this is my wife, Mozzarella…"

Nilla's squeak ended my fantasy. "Crafts. Isn't that the second half of 'arts and crafts'?"

Nonfiction replied, "Yes, it is."

I squeaked, "The children do both!"

Nilla added, "They could sell their creations!"

Economics looked skeptical. "They'd have to sell an awful lot of arts and crafts to raise enough money for all those repairs."

A happy thought stirred in me. The children would not have to work alone. I said, "Maybe they can—if all the kindly critters in Crittertown help!"

Nonfiction patted my shoulder. "You can count on the library colony."

Every mouse started squeaking ideas for crafts.

Cookbooks suggested, "The children can sell baked goods. Everyone loves homemade cookies!"

Magazines added, "The Christmas season's on the way. They can make ornaments and wreaths. People spend tons of money decorating their nests."

General History jumped in. "We can gather

pinecones and balsam branches for wreaths."

He turned to his scouts. "We'll send patrols into the woods and set up relay stations for bringing the supplies back to base."

Magazines said, "We can help make things, too—bend wires, hold things in place while glue dries, and that sort of thing."

At the height of the excitement, Cookbooks squeaked, "Shh! I smell ca…"

Before she could finish that dreaded word, Dot jumped into the center of the gathering. Panicked mice scattered in all directions.

"This way!" General History shouted.

Grayson, Nilla, and I followed him into a narrow alley between piles of old books. Nilla's eyes were black pits of panic. Her chest heaved as she slunk deeper into the shadows.

I peered over General History's shoulder to watch the last of the colony mice scramble for shelter. Poor Cookbooks! Her nose might be quick, but her chubby legs were slow.

She ran toward an old filing cabinet, and a huge white paw blocked her way! Dot's amber eyes glowed like twin flames branding my soul with fear.

Cookbooks turned toward a bag labeled "book sale." As she took off, the cat raised her other paw—to strike or just to tease? We'll never know, because just then, the basement echoed with a loud "Woof! Woof! WOOF!"

Dot's tail instantly fluffed to triple its normal width. I'd never seen anything like it! The cat raced upstairs in a blur of fur.

Cookbooks sighed. "That was a close call!"

Nilla chuckled. "Three cheers for Buttercup!"

"Hip, hip, hooray!" the library mice cheered.

Grayson turned to Nonfiction. "Thank you for your help."

I took a last, wistful look at Poetry and then squeaked, "That's our ride. Good-bye for now."

She said, "Parting is such sweet sorrow."

Nilla groaned. "What does *that* mean?"

I smiled. "I have no idea, but I'm sure it's poetry."

Chapter 4 **Many Paws Make Light Work**

As soon as we climbed onto Buttercup's neck, Nilla patted his ear and squeaked, "You were great!"

Grayson asked, "Why do cat's tails fuzz up like that?"

Buttercup laughed. "It's supposed to make them look bigger and scarier."

Nilla shuddered. "As if cats need to look scarier."

I changed the subject to happier thoughts. "The library colony sure had lots of good ideas!" I was eager to get somewhere less bouncy to write them all down.

51

Buttercup had some ideas, too. "The kids can sell doggie gift baskets and treats! One of the guests gave me a basket once. Mrs. Hill thought it was 'a complete waste of money.' But it was super!"

He barked on. "How about fancy bird feeders? People buy lots of bird feeders. I love to watch the chickadees. Can you imagine hanging upside down to eat?"

Grayson chuckled. "You'd break the branch if you tried to eat in a tree."

Nilla squeaked, "Suet is yummy! Seeds are good, too."

I concluded, "But nothing beats cheese!"

The next morning, as always, Chitchat stopped by the post office on his way to school.

Instead of my usual short note for the kids,
I gave him a long scroll.

Chitchat teased, "What's this? The complete memoirs of a mouse?"

I gave him two acorns. "An extra nut for the added weight."

But I knew what the nosy squirrel really wanted. So I told him, "It's a list of fundraising ideas."

I started to tie the scroll around his neck. But Chitchat said, "Read it to me first."

I sighed. Human postal carriers are paid money to deliver mail. The Critter Post pays Chitchat in acorns—and gossip.

After he heard the list, Chitchat said, "Get your pencil! You need to add squirrel feeders, peanut butter pinecones, and garden gnomes."

While I wrote, Chitchat asked, "Did I ever tell you about the time I escaped from a cat by posing like a garden gnome?"

"Only a few times. Why don't you tell me again after you deliver this list to the kids?"

I wish I could've been there when the third graders read my letter. Instead, Chitchat scurried back to tell me later that morning. The squirrel gushed, "The kids were so excited that they didn't notice Mrs. Olson come into the room. So she took your letter right out of Tanya's hands!"

"Oh no!" I squeaked.

Chitchat laughed. "Oh yes! She'd never seen anything like your tiny paw-writing. But then she read it and asked the kids, 'May I show this list to Principal Clark and Mrs. Brann? I think

54

an arts and crafts sale is a great idea!'"

I asked, "What'd the kids say?"

"They said, 'Sure!'" Chitchat replied. "They were so relieved she hadn't focused on the mystery of the tiny writing."

I was, too!

Chitchat added, "Then Mrs. Olson went to Mr. Clark's office to 'make this thing happen in a big way!'"

I decided to do the same thing. I wrote a letter inviting "all kindly critters" to help with the fair. The trouble, though, was figuring out how to make enough copies.

Just then Charlton, one of the Critter Post recruits, came up to me and asked, "What're you doing?"

The recruits were too young to make

deliveries, so they spent their time learning street names as well as odd and even numbers, and practicing their writing. I grinned and said, "Charlie, I hope your recruits are ready to get busy!"

Soon, even the youngest were copying the invitation. Some of their letters looked more like scribbles than words. But I praised them for their efforts and hid the sloppy ones under my nest.

When Grayson woke from his morning nap he asked, "What's all this?"

He looked at the letters. "At this rate, you'll never have enough to send to every nest in town." Then he grinned slyly. "But there is a way!"

Grayson's ideas scare me. I still shudder when I recall the time I helped him trip a trap.

So with a dry mouth and a nervous stomach I asked, "What do you mean?"

"The copy machine!" Grayson squeaked. "I've seen Mike use it lots of times. You put what you want to copy on the glass, type a number, then push 'copy.'"

I said, "We'll have to wait until Mike goes to lunch."

"Of course," Grayson agreed.

I taped twelve of the neatest invitations to a piece of paper to make one sheet as big as the glass plate. As soon as Mike left, Grayson and I slipped this page under the post office's back door.

Mike had turned off the radio. The office was very quiet as we crawled toward the copy machine. It took two of us to lift the lid.

Grayson grunted, "Put it facedown on the glass."

I looked from him to the paper and grunted back, "With what?" I thought of Nilla napping in her nest. We should have woken her. Clearly this was a three-mouse job!

But Grayson doesn't give up. He stretched a foot toward the page. I stretched out a foot also. Between the two of us, we managed to turn the sheet over and center it on the glass.

My paws ached from holding the lid over our heads. It reminded me of a trap! I dreaded getting squashed under it and being photographed dozens of times while the life leaked out of me.

As soon as we released the lid, it fell with an awful bang. We froze, but no one heard the noise.

Grayson tapped the "copy" key. Nothing happened.

"What's wrong?" I asked.

Grayson shrugged. "I don't know!" He jumped on the key with both feet. Suddenly, we heard the familiar whirr and saw the bright light flash under the glass.

"Cover your eyes!" I squeaked, putting my paws over my face. I peeked through my fingers and saw Grayson staring into the light.

"We did it!" he exclaimed as a sheet of paper oozed onto the tray. "Now for twenty more!" Grayson tapped the number keys. "Do you think twenty is enough?"

Nilla would've tried to do the math: twelve invitations on each page times twenty copies. Instead, I looked at the stack and said, "Let's get these on their way. We can always make more."

We were halfway to the door when I shouted, "The original is still on the glass!" We scrambled back to retrieve it. With my heart pounding with panic, I wondered what Mike would think if he found our invitations.

Back in the basement, the Critter Post recruits helped Grayson, Nilla, and me chew the big pages into single invitations. Then we rolled up each one with string to tie around a mail carrier's neck.

Nilla scolded. "I can't believe you didn't wake me!"

Grayson shrugged. "What's that human expression—'you snooze, you lose'?"

Nilla got so mad that she chewed right into an invitation. Grayson laughed.

All the Critter Post carriers were eager to help with this special delivery. Birds, chipmunks, and squirrels spread the word around town so fast that I could hardly believe it!

Before the school day was over, pinecones and other craft supplies started pouring in. Birds brought old feathers, certain that "the children can think of a use for them."

Some generous squirrels even parted with acorns. Not Rusty, of course. He still thought the whole campaign was "pure foolishness."

I couldn't wait to share the good news with the kids. But Buttercup was late!

Grayson grumbled, "Where is that silly dog?"

"I see him!" Nilla squeaked.

"What's that behind him?" Grayson asked.

The Lab pulled something large and red. Grayson and I recognized it at the same time. We squeaked in unison, "A wagon!"

Buttercup tugged the wagon's handle and stumbled around its bulk.

I said, "No wonder he's late."

Buttercup dropped the handle long enough to bark, "Sorry I'm late." Then he bumbled

toward us again. When he reached the post office, Buttercup explained, "Chitchat told me about all the supplies. So I figured I better bring the wagon." Then he added, "The children make it look easy to pull. But it's hard!"

By the time the wagon was loaded, we were so late that Jill and Bill came to us.

"There you are!" Bill exclaimed.

Jill added, "We were starting to worry!"

Then they saw the wagon heaped with pinecones, balsam boughs, acorns, and more. With the twins' help, we soon reached April's garage.

The kids were amazed at all the supplies the Crittertown critters had already gathered. Tanya declared, "This is going to be awesome!"

Everyone started working right away. The kids quickly learned that Magazines was right. Not to brag, but having mouse helpers makes crafts go much quicker.

Tiny paws easily arrange balsam branches to form wreaths. And we're good at turning Popsicle sticks and other craft supplies into Christmas ornaments.

Jane said, "It's too bad you can't be with us in art class."

Hannah agreed. "I think Mrs. Brann would like you."

Grayson hesitated. But I shook my head and wrote, "Too risky." Then I added, "Remember when Principal Clark called the exterminator?" I also remembered him calling me "vermin."

April sighed. "It's too bad grown-ups can't know you the way we do."

Javier added, "Just imagine if people and mice all over the world started working together. Think of the things we could build! I bet you guys would be great at making computers, with all those tiny circuits and switches…" His voice trailed off, and he started sketching.

"He's off again," Bill observed. "On another one of his nutty ideas."

I wondered, was it nutty? Besides, what's wrong with nutty? I love nuts, especially roasted acorns! Think of all the lives that could be saved if people stopped hating mice. Instead of building traps, we could build things together. Maybe even spaceships like the one that went to the moon. I know it isn't really made of cheese, but…what a vision!

We worked until April's mother said it was time to go home. The children were very proud of all the things they made in just one afternoon.

Tanya declared, "This is going to be the best crafts sale ever!" and everyone cheered.

Chapter 5　*A Dark Rumor*

That night Grayson, Nilla, and I felt too excited to stay in the basement. Grayson begged his grandfather to let us make a quick Dumpster run.

Brownback agreed. "As long as the Postmouseter goes along to keep you from turning this 'quick run' into a grand tour."

We weren't even halfway to the big, blue metal container when we heard someone chattering in the tree overhanging the parking lot. Chitchat had "big news!"

Grayson was skeptical. "That gossip thought it was 'big news' when Mike got a new car."

I thought the postmaster's car was big news, too. But I didn't feel like arguing with Grayson. Luckily, I didn't have to because Nilla piped up. "Let's at least hear him out."

Without waiting for Grayson's reply, she rushed off to meet Chitchat. Grayson and I followed.

Grayson said, "So what's your 'big news'?"

Chitchat glared at him. "Well if you're going to take that tone…"

Nilla smiled. "Don't mind him, Chitchat. I'm dying to know, and so is Cheddar."

Chitchat scrambled down from the tree so he could stand close to us. He looked over both shoulders before he began. "I just heard this from old Rusty, who lives in the woods behind the library."

Grayson groaned. "Oh, that old crank." Grayson was still sore from the scolding Rusty gave us the first day we visited the library. We took some acorns from the old squirrel's pantry, and he called us a bunch of nasty names.

Chitchat frowned. "Rusty may be cranky, but he's no fool. He overheard a meeting of some of the younger members of the library colony. It seems they'd been gathering under his tree for a while, and this morning Rusty heard them talking about war."

Grayson suddenly snapped to attention. "War with whom?"

Chitchat smirked. "Wouldn't you like to know!"

For a moment, I feared Grayson might be foolish enough to try to fight a squirrel. But with great effort, he calmed himself enough to say, "I'm sorry I doubted you, Chitchat. This is vital news, and we appreciate your bringing it to us."

Chitchat barely waited for Grayson to finish his apology before he gushed, "With you! With the post office colony! The library's gotten quite crowded, and General History thinks the post office would make a 'more secure headquarters.'"

Grayson said, "The library was awfully crowded last night. But how could General History think that we'd just let them take our territory?"

I looked over at Nilla. She seemed greener than the time we ate some spoiled sardines. "What's wrong?" I asked.

She shook her head. Her eyes filled with tears.

Grayson turned to her. "What is it?"

Nilla covered her face with her paws and moaned. "I told him."

"You told what to whom?" Grayson asked.

"I told General History…everything!" Nilla wailed. "While every mouse was squeaking about ways to save the school, he took me in the corner and asked me a whole bunch of questions, like how many mice are in our colony and who guards the entrance holes."

Grayson yelled, "How could you be so foolish? What were you thinking?"

Nilla wiped at her tears. "I…" Her voice sank to a whisper. "I thought he…liked me. And that he was just asking all those questions so he'd have an excuse to talk to me." She broke into full sobs.

I patted her shoulder.

Grayson fumed. "You told the enemy general all our most vital data!"

"I didn't think he was our enemy," Nilla wailed. "I thought…" her voice trailed off.

"I understand," I said. "The library colony has been so nice to us. It's almost as if they were part of our colony."

Grayson frowned. "But they're not! And now…"

Nilla broke into fresh sobs.

I couldn't stand to see her suffer. So I told Grayson, "Please don't be so hard on Nilla. Who knows what you would have told Poetry if she asked you?"

Grayson opened his mouth to argue but stopped himself. Instead, he just punched his fist into his other paw. "Traps, poison, and brooms!" he cursed. "You're probably right. In any case, what's done is done."

I nodded my head toward Nilla and whispered to Grayson, "Don't tell me, tell her."

Grayson sighed. He put one paw on Nilla's shoulder. "It's not your fault."

She cried harder and then sniffled. "Yes it is! But what can we do about it?"

Chitchat yawned. "Sorry. I know you mice love to stay up all night. But squirrels prefer waking with the sun. I should've been in my nest hours ago."

Grayson grumbled. "But you couldn't wait to tell us the bad news."

"What was that?" Chitchat challenged.

Grayson shook his head. "I'm sorry,

nothing—just me worrying out loud. Thank you for staying up late to keep us informed."

He sounded so much like his grandfather that I half expected to see white hairs on his muzzle.

Chitchat yawned again. "I'll see you tomorrow." He started to leave.

Nilla called after him. "Please…don't tell anyone else what a fool I've been."

Chitchat turned around and shook his head. "You're no more a fool than the rest of us—just young and in love."

Nilla looked horrified. "I am not!"

Grayson turned away so Nilla wouldn't see him chuckle.

I shrugged. "It's all right, Nilla. Your secret's safe with us, right Chitchat?"

The squirrel nodded. "I won't tell anyone! Not even if they pulled my tail and threw me in a dog kennel."

"Thanks," Nilla said, as Chitchat scampered up the tree trunk and vanished among rattling twigs.

We made a quick check of the Dumpster. We found several treasures, including a whole cheese wedge that wasn't even moldy—just past its "best if sold by" date.

I was so pleased with this find that I spoke without thinking. "No wonder the library colony wants our territory. I bet they never find treats like this!"

Nilla's miserable expression made me wish I'd kept my cheese-loving mouth shut.

Grayson looked annoyed, too.

"I'm sorry," I said. But it was too late.

Nilla sighed. "It doesn't matter. We're going to have to face the truth sooner or later."

"We don't have to tell Pops the whole story," Grayson began. "We'll just say that we 'heard a group inside the library colony plans to attack,' and 'we have reason to believe they may know about our defenses.'"

Nilla looked grateful, but also doubtful. "Won't he wonder about that 'reason to believe'?"

Grayson shrugged. "We'll say our source didn't know how they knew about our defenses. After all, it could just be a chatty cricket or a nosy mole."

Nilla grinned. "That's right. I'm not the only one around here who has a big mouth and a small brain."

I chuckled. "Your brain is fine. You're even learning math!"

Grayson smiled. "Okay, so that's what we'll tell Pops. Then we can start building up our defenses. More guards, more patrols, maybe some new weapons."

I could tell Grayson felt excited. War would give him a chance to prove himself as a leader.

But I felt miserable. I didn't want to fight

Poetry's colony. I didn't want to risk my life—
or take someone else's. There had to be
another way!

Arriving with a whole wedge of cheese
made us heroes. Every mouse in the colony
scrambled for a bite.

I felt too heartsick to be hungry—even
for cheese! Besides, we were busy. As soon as
Grayson said, "We have news," his grandfather
led the three of us into his nest.

Nilla hardly asked any questions. In fact,
she was so quiet that Brownback asked, "Are
you all right, my dear?"

"Just tired," she fibbed.

Grayson distracted his grandfather with
plans for patrols and new weapons.

Brownback sighed. "That's all good strategy," he told Grayson. "But if it's only a small group within the library colony that wants war…"

I jumped on this opening. "Then maybe we can make a treaty instead!"

Brownback nodded. "That's what I was thinking."

"Nonfiction may not want to go to war, either," I gushed. "After all, he once said you were 'a mouse after his own heart.'"

Brownback looked alarmed. "Why would I want his heart?"

Nilla giggled. "Another crazy human expression that's not as nasty as it sounds. It just means you're like him and he's like you, or something like that."

I nodded. "His grandson, General History, is the one who wants war. If we can offer Nonfiction another way to solve the library colony's overcrowding problem..."

Brownback started pacing as he finished my thought. "That would be much better than risking lives and wasting resources in a war." He reached the wall of his nest and turned around to face us. "Grayson, why don't you move ahead with building up our defenses? It can't hurt to be prepared. Double the guard at each hole, and change the schedule so the guards serve shorter shifts. We need them to be extra alert!"

Grayson rushed to obey. Here was his chance to strut around and give orders!

His grandfather called after him, "And make

a list of all our weapons. Before we start to make more, we need to know what we have."

Grayson groaned. Tidying the storeroom and counting weapons didn't sound like fun. But he knew better than to argue when "Pops" was in such a serious mood.

Once Grayson was on his way, Brownback turned to Nilla and me. "I think you two are better suited to the task of writing a treaty between our colony and the library." He winked at Nilla. "Since you're becoming so good at math, you can help Cheddar number each clause."

"What's a clause?" Nilla asked. "Does it have anything to do with Santa?"

I smiled. Nilla must be all right. She was back to asking questions!

Chapter 6 *Negative Numbers*

The next morning, Grayson, Nilla, and I sneaked up to the post office after the carriers left on their routes. I hoped the clerk had brought in more toasted pumpkin seeds. Mike and the carriers didn't like the seeds much, but

"somehow" they kept disappearing anyway.

(Ha, ha!)

The seeds weren't nearly as good as cheese, but they made a fine snack. And we had grown quite fond of the quiet mornings at the post office, listening to Mike's radio and catching up on town gossip.

That morning the school secretary came to buy three rolls of stamps. Mike was surprised. The secretary explained that Principal Clark was inspired by the children's letter-writing campaign. "He's writing to the alumni and summer people. He thinks lots of people will want to keep Crittertown from losing its school."

Nilla squeaked, "What's alumni?"

Grayson and I had seen that word on many pieces of mail. "Alumni associations" were always mailing things about school events like fundraisers.

I explained, "Alumni are people who graduated from a certain school."

Nilla nodded, then asked, "What's graduated?"

We went on like that for most of the morning. I was glad when Mike's lunch hour finally arrived. We filled an envelope with pumpkin seeds and slipped some newspapers out of the recycling bin to carry back to the colony.

As always, Brownback insisted on "right of first reading" of the newspapers, before any mouse could tear them up for nesting. He found an article about the "school budget crisis" that made him frown.

Grayson asked, "What is it, Pops?"

Brownback shook his head. "The numbers are too big," he began. "The cost of repairing Crittertown Elementary School…it's way more money than the children can raise selling wreaths, pot holders, and brownies."

Nilla sighed. "I was afraid of that. Too many zeroes! If they're really 'nothing,' why can't we just subtract a few to make things right?"

Grayson and Brownback looked at me. I told Nilla, "I'll explain it later." Then I muttered to myself, "At least I'll try." Math isn't nearly as interesting to me as cheese. Did you know that humans in countries around the world make their own special kinds of cheese? And not just from cow's milk—they use milk from goats, buffaloes, even camels! Look it up—you'll be amazed.

The rest of the news was the usual mix of natural disasters, wars, fashion, and celebrity gossip. I asked Brownback to let me chew out an article about a peace treaty. I wanted some idea of what might persuade the library colony not to attack.

Just thinking about that huge task made me realize how tired I was. So I took a nap until Buttercup arrived to bring us to April's garage for after-school fun.

As Nilla and I followed Grayson to the hole, he turned and whispered, "Don't say anything about the war with the library colony."

Nilla asked, "Why not?"

Grayson sighed. "Because if there really is going to be a war...well..."

Nilla looked down at her paws. I hoped she

wouldn't cry again. Tears wouldn't dissolve her mistake with General History.

I said, "I guess it's better not to involve the children or anyone else who might get hurt or… say something to our…" I couldn't bring myself to call the library colony our "enemy." But we all knew what I meant.

Buttercup must've smelled something, because all the way to April's garage, the dog kept asking questions: "What's wrong? Is someone sick? Did you lose your favorite toy?"

Finally, Grayson fibbed. "Oh, we're just feeling bad because Brownback did the math, and he thinks the children's crafts can't save the school."

Buttercup grumbled. "Why do humans care so much about numbers? You can't eat them.

You can't smell them. You can't chase them. What's the point?"

Nilla agreed. "I've been studying math. And I'm getting better at things like carrying ones and multiplying. But I still don't see why humans think numbers are so important."

And so they chattered for the rest of the journey. Meanwhile, I tried to memorize every tree, mailbox, and driveway, because it occurred to me that if Brownback was right and the school closed, then everything might change. I wanted to preserve each detail of our after-school routine against the day when we might no longer make this pleasant trip.

I thought seeing the children would cheer me up. But the third graders felt just as gloomy as we did. Brownback wasn't the only one who'd been "doing the math." Mrs. Olson put a long division problem on the blackboard. It showed the amount of money needed to fix the school divided by the number of people in Crittertown. When the children had finally solved the problem, they realized that the crafts fair was not a good solution—unless they could somehow sell over $200 worth of cookies, key holders, and birdhouses to each family in town!

Tanya imitated Mrs. Olson's voice. "I'm sorry. I didn't mean to discourage you. I just thought you ought to know what you're up against."

Tanya used her own voice to wail, "We're up against the wall! But we can't quit."

April said something in her usual whisper. Javier leaned close and repeated, "Her father says, 'when you're up against the wall, draw a door.'"

90

Javier looked puzzled. Then he drew a rectangle in his sketchbook and sketched a doorknob in the middle. He ripped out the page and handed it to April. "Here's your door. But I don't think it's going to do us much good."

April hid her mouth as she laughed softly. "It doesn't work like that, but... thanks."

Jill said, "I think what April's dad means is, we just need to keep trying!" She looked around the crowded garage. "After all, what else are we going to do with all these pinecones and Popsicle sticks?"

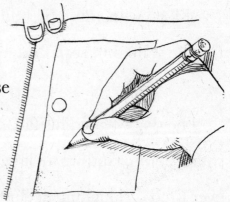

Everyone laughed, and most of the children took that as the signal to start making something. But Tanya said, "That's a good question, Jill. What *are* we going to make with all this stuff? I say we go to the library for some fresh ideas. There might be some new crafts magazines on the shelves by now."

I knew there were, because the librarian had picked some up that morning. Normally, I'd be eager for a chance to glimpse Poetry. But knowing that we might soon be at war...

"I'll go with you," Jill told Tanya. "I could use the walk. I'm sure Buttercup feels the same way."

The dog wagged his tail so hard that his butt wagged, too. And we all laughed. None of us ever tired of laughing at Buttercup's butt.

Bill didn't want to go to the library. "I'd rather just build stuff." The other boys decided to stay, too.

Jane scooped me up and put me in her pocket. "I know Cheddar will want to come. He loves the library."

I would've squeaked "no" or written a note to that effect. But Grayson squeaked first. "See what you can find out, Cheddar. No one will suspect you."

I wondered if I should feel insulted. Why wouldn't anyone "suspect" me—because everyone knows I'm a scaredy-mouse? I chose not to think about that. I simply agreed. "All right. But I don't even know what to look for."

"Just keep your eyes and ears open," Grayson squeaked. "Look for anything different. Listen to whatever's going on. I'm counting on you—and so is Pops."

Jane started to lift Nilla, too, but she scampered out of the girl's hand. Jane shrugged. "I guess Nilla doesn't want to go."

Grayson busied himself bending some wire. So Tanya said, "Looks like Grayson and Nilla want to stay here with the boys." She patted Nilla's head with the tip of her finger and then added, "We'll be back soon."

As we were leaving, I saw April use a thumbtack to stick Javier's drawing of a door up on one of the plywood walls.

He asked, "What are you doing?"

April giggled. "I don't know, really. I just thought it might lead us somewhere good."

Chapter 7   *Library Spy*

On the way to the library, I scribbled a note on a gum wrapper I found in Jane's pocket. It said,

Doing some research. Don't worry about me.

Then I signed it with,

Just keep thinking…happy thoughts!

Cheddar

As Jane read the note to the other girls, I slipped off to the basement. I lingered in the narrow passage, listening to the sounds of the colony.

Many mice softly snored. Some cleaned their nests. I also heard the peaceful sound of pages being turned. Thanks to all the book sale donations, the library colony always had plenty of things to read, even without going upstairs.

I sniffed the air. Something was different. There was a fiery smell, but it wasn't at all like Cookbooks' roasted acorns.

I wasn't the only one sniffing. I heard Cookbooks herself announce, "I smell…"

Every mouse held its breath, dreading the word "cat." Instead, Cookbooks concluded "…foreign mouse" just as I stepped into the basement.

She saw me and smiled. "It isn't a stranger. It's Cheddar!"

Cookbooks patted me with one of her plump paws. "We didn't know you were coming. But give me a minute, and I'll whip up a snack."

"It's all right," I said. "I just tagged along with the children. They came to get more craft project ideas."

Cookbooks shrugged. "Recipes for making things you can't eat. Decorations. Toys. Lots of humans like that stuff. I don't see why. If I'm going to spend time making something, I want to be able to eat it."

Poetry laughed her wonderful, musical laugh. "Some people prefer things that are more permanent than pie."

Cookbooks shrugged again. "I suppose it's a matter of taste."

Poetry said, "My grandfather is napping. But I know he'll want to see you—especially if you have any news."

"No news!" I said quickly. "Just visiting with the kids."

I looked all around the basement. In the daylight, it was nearly as shabby as the post office cellar. But the stacks of books everywhere gave it a certain charm.

Without being too obvious, I tried to locate the source of that strange smell. It seemed to be coming from the hot water heater.

I scurried over there. At my approach, several soldiers suddenly gathered to form a furry wall between the large machine and me.

"Is everything all right?" I strained to see through the gaps between their broad shoulders. I glimpsed General History and several other young males bent over some kind of oven. Their faces glowed from the heat.

They wore heavy mittens to protect their paws.

Poetry caught up with me. "Don't mind my rude brother and his friends. They are…"

One of the soldiers broke ranks and placed his paw over Poetry's mouth. "It's nothing," the soldier said. "Nothing wrong. Nothing to concern you."

General History looked up from his task. "Cheddar? What are you doing here?"

He glared briefly at his soldiers before changing his expression to a stiff smile. "No one told me we had…visitors."

"Only me," I said. "Just wanted to say hello while the children do some research upstairs." Then I added, "I thought I smelled something cooking. But I guess I was wrong."

General History laughed nervously. "Oh, no! Just some…metallurgy."

"Metallurgy?" I asked.

"A hobby," General History said. "Making things out of metal, like jewelry and lamps."

"That sounds interesting!" I exclaimed. "May I see?"

General History stepped forward and took my paw. Behind him the soldiers reformed their tight line, once again blocking my view.

"Nothing much to look at," he said. "And you don't want to singe your fur. Shall we see if grandfather's awake?"

I assured General History that I had no news, and therefore there was no need to wake Nonfiction. When Poetry started to talk to me, two of the soldiers intruded.

I tried to sound casual when I told her, "If you ever want to visit or write to me, just tell Chitchat to tell Buttercup. He likes visiting here because it gives him a chance to fuzz up Dot's tail."

Poetry smiled. And it looked even more beautiful than the sun breaking through clouds. "Thanks, Cheddar. Maybe I will. It's about time I saw more of this town."

The grim presence of the staring soldiers

cast a shadow over both of us. So we said nothing more.

I felt the soldiers' eyes on me, even after I squeezed through the passage. I thought about trying to sneak into the library to be with the children. But knowing that Dot lurked in there made me decide to wait outside with Buttercup.

I told him Poetry might visit the post office. Buttercup winked at me. "You're sweet on her, aren't you? I can tell just by the way you say her name, like it's a song."

I laughed.

"What's so funny?" he asked.

I explained, "The words to a song *are* poetry." I felt my cheeks grow hot as I admitted, "Yes, I do think she's the prettiest mouse I've ever seen. But…" My voice trailed off. What could Poetry possibly see in me?

So I simply concluded, "Anyway, I hope it's all right that I told her you'd be willing to give her a lift."

"Any time!" Buttercup replied. "You know how much I enjoy teasing Dot."

I laughed.

Buttercup ran to the nearest window and barked. Bow wow wow, WOOF!

Jill rushed out the door. "Shh, Buttercup! You scared the library cat."

Buttercup wagged his tail, and Jill patted his head. "I suppose you can't help it. You just don't know any better."

Buttercup and I waited until Jill went back in the library to burst out laughing.

We spent the rest of the afternoon helping the children with their crafts. Nilla and I found that we could weave pot holders super fast by turning it into a kind of dance. It was fun!

When Buttercup left the garage to play catch with Bill and Wyatt, Grayson asked me what I'd learned at the library. I described General History's strange "hobby."

"What do you think it means?" Nilla wondered.

Grayson frowned. "They must be making weapons!"

"Out of what?" Nilla asked.

Grayson's frown deepened. "Did you see a source for metal?"

I closed my eyes and tried to remember everything I'd seen behind the soldiers. "Yes!" I suddenly squeaked. "I saw a box of 'jumbo paper clips.'"

Grayson started pacing. "They must be

melting the tips of the paper clips to sharpen them into swords, arrows, and spears!"

I shuddered.

But Grayson smiled. "Good work, Cheddar. Did you find out anything else?"

Before I could answer, Jane asked, "What's all the squeaking about?"

Jill handed me her assignment pad. I felt guilty lying to such nice children. But I had my "orders." So I wrote, "Nothing much. Just the crafts."

Jill looked skeptical. "Really? Then why did you stop working?"

"Yes," Jane teased. "Look at all April's done while you've been squeaking."

April blushed. Then she said softly, "I call them 'imagination doors.'" She added, "You can put them anywhere you want your mind to wander." She had used Popsicle sticks, twine, and tiny acorns to make several small doors. Instead of a house number or name, each one had a label like "the future," "precious memories," or my favorite, "happy thoughts."

"I think they're great!" Tanya declared. "You could use them in a dollhouse, or just put them on a wall, your locker, a tree—anywhere."

"I bet we sell a bunch of these at the fair," Hannah said.

So we all started making "imagination doors." Coming up with different labels for them was fun.

At least it would have been if my mind hadn't kept wandering to scary places. What if we did get into a war with the library colony?

What if they really were making weapons far worse than anything our colony had?

"Why don't you write a label?" Jane prompted me.

"Yes, Cheddar. You have such neat little handwriting." Jill rolled a pen toward me.

I lifted the pen and held it over a square of bright paper trimmed with toothpicks. Where did I want my imagination to go? What door did I want to open?

"What's he writing?" Javier asked.

Andy guessed, "I bet it says, 'cheese store.'"

"Or 'the moon,'" Bill chimed in. "Cheddar likes to think the moon really is made of green cheese."

"What're you talking about?" Ian asked.

"Haven't you heard the old jokes about

the moon being made of green cheese?" Jill replied.

"It's because the moon looks lumpy, like cheese curds before they've hardened into ripe cheese," Bill added. "Cheese makers call unripe cheese green, like green tomatoes."

"So there's no cheese that's really green?" Javier sounded disappointed.

"Right," Bill said. "And the moon isn't made of cheese."

Javier laughed. "Duh!"

Jane looked up from Cheddar's writing. "It starts with a 'P.'"

My body blocked the rest of the letters, so the children couldn't read the label until I finished. I stepped back to make sure I'd spelled it right.

"Peace," April read aloud in her sweet, soft voice.

"Peace," Javier repeated loud enough for the other children to hear.

"That's very nice," Nilla squeaked.

Grayson shook his head. "Yes, 'very nice,' but how do you propose to achieve it?"

Sadly, I had no idea.

Chapter 8 *Opening the Door*

As soon as we reached the post office, Grayson said, "We have to tell Pops about the weapons."

Brownback agreed that secret metallurgy did suggest an arms buildup.

Grayson said, "There are plenty of paper clips at the post office. We just have to figure out how to heat the tips. And if General History can do that, so can we!"

Without waiting for his grandfather to answer, Grayson rushed off to find the best tinkerers in the colony. I started to call after him, but Brownback stopped me. "Let him go, Cheddar. I'd rather talk to you and Nilla."

"Have you made any progress on the treaty yet?" he asked.

I looked down at the floor.

Brownback chuckled. "I know. Peace isn't easy. That's why I thought you might need some help."

He folded his paws behind his back and started pacing. "The first thing we need to do is figure out what both sides want."

He rolled a pencil stub toward me. "Here, take a piece of paper and write 'post office' on one side and 'library' on the other."

When that was done, Brownback said, "We know the library colony needs more territory.

Could we share some of our turf if we received something of equal value in exchange?"

"What's as valuable as territory?" Nilla asked.

"Cheese!" I blurted out. It had been quite a long time since our last meal.

Brownback chuckled. "Write 'food sources' under 'post office' and 'territory' under 'library.'" Then he looked deep in thought. "Does the library colony have any food sources they could share with us?"

Nilla grinned. "There's old Rusty's oak trees! They're full of acorns."

Brownback nodded. "I suppose that's why the colony is getting so crowded. Lots of food means lots of babies. Well…now we're getting somewhere."

Brownback, Nilla, and I spent all night

talking and writing. Actually, Nilla fell asleep for

a while, but Brownback and I just kept going

until we had a treaty that was longer than the both of us, including our tails!

The treaty spelled out everything (with a few misspellings). In general, it said that the post office colony would be willing to offer some living space to members of the library colony in exchange for the freedom to harvest food off library colony land.

We proposed merging the colonies for our mutual benefit. Females could raise litters in the safety of the post office, away from Dot's evening friskies. Young mice ready to learn various subjects could live under the library in a sort of boarding school.

The double colony could have a combined "army" of scouts to patrol the borders and seek new food sources—and make contact with other colonies who might be willing to enter into a treaty.

Resources like the post office colony's newspapers and the library colony's access to facts would be shared.

The leaders of both colonies would become co-leaders of the merged colony. If they couldn't agree on an issue, it would be decided by a vote. Any mouse old enough to have a nest would be allowed to vote.

My writing paw felt tired. Brownback yawned and said, "Read it back to me again, please."

I was up to the part about the "combined army" when Twitchy raced into Brownback's nest.

"Visitors!" he exclaimed. Then he ran back

to the entrance and said, "Sorry! I forgot to knock."

"Come in," Brownback told him.

Twitchy ran in, ran back out, knocked, and ran back in again. "Visitors from the library colony!"

Brownback smoothed his fur as Twitchy went on. "It's that girl, the pretty one you told me about. And a tall, skinny lady named Travel. They're waiting at the entrance. Should I bring them here or tell them to wait for you out there?"

Twitchy danced from one foot to the other. Brownback patted Twitchy's shoulder as he walked past him. Brownback then turned to me and said, "Let's greet our guests."

I smoothed my fur and then followed. Poetry

was here! I wondered what she wanted. I hoped she wanted to see me!

I vaguely remembered Travel from our first evening at the library colony. When Brownback bowed, she said, "Enchanté!" She added, "That's French for 'enchanted.'"

Nilla asked, "Why is she enchanted? I thought that meant magical. Is she a witch?"

Poetry blessed us with one of her beautiful smiles. "It's an expression that's short for 'enchanted to meet you,' meaning, 'it's nice to meet you'—only fancier."

Nilla rolled her eyes. "Just what we needed, another confusing expression!"

Poetry explained that Nonfiction thought "a young lady" needed an escort when she went visiting. And Travel seemed the logical choice.

Travel couldn't wait to "see the sights, meet the natives," and "learn the local customs."

Poetry told Brownback that she was acting as her grandfather's ambassador. Nilla, of course, wanted to know "What's an ambassador?"

Brownback confused her more when he said, "A diplomat who represents one country or group when visiting another."

Nilla asked, "What's a diplomat?" just as Grayson appeared. He was surprised to see our guests.

Brownback suggested that Grayson give Travel "the grand tour." Grayson said, "What about Poetry?"

His grandfather replied, "Cheddar, Nilla, and I will take care of Poetry."

Grayson started to protest, "Aw, Pops…"

But Travel latched on to one of his paws and asked, "What do the locals do for fun around here?"

Brownback led Poetry to his nest. He told her about the treaty. She promised to bring it directly to Nonfiction. She assured us that he wanted peace. Then she added, "The problem is my stubborn brother. He and his soldiers are so excited about fighting a war. Grandfather is afraid he won't be able to stop them!"

Brownback looked over his shoulder at Grayson and whispered, "We have a similar problem. But I think we might borrow a solution from the humans."

Brownback asked Poetry if she'd heard of the Olympics. He suggested that the colonies hold a "Mouselympics" to let "the young hotshots" have a chance to show off while running races, jumping, throwing, and competing in other sporting events. He concluded, "The winners could become the leaders of the combined colony's army."

Poetry smiled. "I believe you're as smart as my grandfather!"

I took out a piece of paper and started writing. "We can make the Mouselympics an amendment to the treaty."

Nilla asked, "What's an amendment?"

And we all laughed.

Travel declared the post office colony "charming and rustic." When I gave her some of the clerk's toasted pumpkin seeds, she added, "The local cuisine is delicious!"

Grayson said, "Wait until you taste the cheese crackers." He glanced at me. "It's too bad those don't ever seem to last around Cheddar."

I blushed. Then Grayson noticed the roll of paper tied with a ribbon that Poetry held like a leash.

"It's a letter for Nonfiction," she said. Then she giggled. "Does this make me an official Critter Post carrier?"

"Of course!" I exclaimed.

Grayson looked suspicious, but what could he do?

Brownback said, "Please give your grandfather our regards."

Poetry replied, "I'd like to come back and take the grand tour, too." She smiled at Grayson, and the clouds left his face.

As soon as Poetry and Travel were gone, Grayson wanted to know what we had talked about in Brownback's nest.

"Mostly about the Mouselympics," Brownback replied.

"The mouse-whatics?" Grayson asked.

"It's explained in the letter we sent to Nonfiction," Brownback began. "If he agrees, our colonies will compete in a day of sporting events. Cheddar thinks the children will be happy to help, as long as we schedule it after the crafts fair."

"Mouselympics!" Grayson exclaimed. "Are there prizes for the winners?"

"I suppose we'll need to get some," Brownback answered.

Grayson grinned. "This'll be great! I wonder how many prizes I'll win..."

Brownback winked at me. When I was sure Grayson wasn't looking, I winked back.

Chapter 9   *"Mouseletes" in Training*

I had just settled in for a nice morning nap when I heard someone approach my nest. "Rise and shine, Cheddar! The mail truck just left."

I rolled over and muttered sleepily. "That's okay. You and Nilla can go upstairs without me."

Grayson asked, "You don't want any cheese crackers?"

At the word "cheese," my eyes popped wide open. Of course I wanted cheese crackers! I wanted them even more than usual, because I was determined to save one to give Poetry.

While I stood up and stretched, Grayson fidgeted. "Come on, sleepyhead!"

"What's the rush?" I asked. "You know it's safer to wait until after the carriers load their cars."

Grayson sighed. "Safer isn't always better. We have work to do. The tinkerers have an idea for making weapons. But they can't test it until I bring them some jumbo paper clips."

My heart sank. With Grayson and General History both so eager for war, did the peace treaty have a chance?

Grayson grew annoyed all over again when Nilla said, "Shouldn't we wait until the carriers leave?"

"Quit worrying," he snapped. "Just stick with me and stay alert."

We were so early that the clerk was still unloading the mail cages. She tossed the packages into big bins for Route 1 and Route 2. She looked surprised when she read the label of an Express Mail package.

When the Route 2 carrier arrived, the clerk said, "You have an Express Mail package for the school from Arthur Kingston. Could it be *the* Arthur Kingston?"

The carrier said, "Who's Arthur Kingston?"

"He's a great artist!" the clerk exclaimed. "He painted lots of book covers and a famous poster of a knight on a hill with these amazing clouds behind it."

The Route 1 carrier called from behind her shelves of mail, "I had that poster!"

The clerk went back to sorting. "It's probably just someone with the same name."

Later that day, when the school secretary

bought stamps, we found out it was *the* Arthur Kingston. She said, "He attended Crittertown Elementary School until his family moved out of state. He didn't graduate in Maine and wasn't born here, so he isn't known as a Maine artist."

Mike listened as the secretary chattered on. "After he received Mr. Clark's letter, Mr. Kingston dug out some drawings he did while he lived in Crittertown—and he's donated them to the school. Principal Clark plans to hold an auction at the crafts fair. He's going to send letters to all the summer people to see if they want to bid on 'the early works of Arthur Kingston.'"

Mike exclaimed, "Well, that's wicked decent of him. I wonder if the auction will raise enough money to repair the school."

The secretary smiled. "I hope so! Because the Lakeville secretary has more years on the job, and a combined school won't need two secretaries."

Mike assured her that even if the schools merged, she would most likely "land on her feet."

"I'm not a cat," the secretary said. "But I suppose I'll manage somehow."

"What does she mean?" Nilla asked.

I'd read in *Cat Fancy* magazine that when cats fall, they usually land on their feet. But what that had to do with the secretary keeping her job or finding another was beyond me.

I suggested, "While Mike's busy, should we get the crackers?"

Grayson chuckled. "Is cheese all you think about?"

I didn't want to admit I was actually thinking of Poetry. I made sure Grayson didn't see me tuck one of the crackers in a plastic bag that used to hold pumpkin seeds. When we went back to the basement, I hid the bag under my nest.

I knew Grayson would soon be busy training for the Mouselympics. He and his more athletic friends had cleared a track around the edge of the basement.

These mouseletes raced around the track until they made the rest of us dizzy! They used pencils and old ledger books to practice pole vaulting. An old ruler measured their progress in the broad jump.

While Grayson was jogging and jumping, I used cardboard and tape to make a box big enough for the cracker. Then I wrote a note to the children about the Mouselympics.

Between races I heard Grayson tell his grandfather, "We don't need a war to beat the library colony!"

Brownback winked at me again.

Grayson asked, "Don't you want to train, too, Cheddar? I know you can run fast."

Nilla chuckled. "You sure sprinted the day we explored the market!"

"That was different," I said, shuddering at the memory. I'd been terrified! "If I'm not running *to* some cheese or *away* from a cat or other danger, it's hard to get my paws moving."

Grayson giggled. "Maybe we need to add a cheese-eating contest."

I smiled. "Now that's an event I could sink my teeth into!" For a moment, I was lost in a cheese-flavored dream.

Then several small paws tugged my attention away from that delicious vision. Charlie and some of the other Critter Post recruits squeaked, "We want to be in the Mouselimpers, too!"

"Mouselympics," I said. "But it's only for grown-ups."

Charlie grumbled. "Everything's only for grown-ups. Can't we help?"

I looked at Grayson. He shrugged and ran off to join the other mouseletes racing around the track.

Charlie asked, "Why aren't you running?"

"Cheddar's too fat," a bony young recruit muttered.

Charlie pulled the skinny mouse's tail—and I didn't stop him. But I did prevent further fighting by saying, "There *is* something important we can all do. Every sporting event needs a cheering crowd. We can make signs and pom-poms to cheer on the post office colony."

I briefly wondered if the recruits would go for this idea, or if they'd insist on holding a junior Mouselympics. Then suddenly my ears filled with high-pitched squeaks. "Yay, Cheddar!" "Yay, us!" "Yay post office colony!"

We spent the rest of the morning turning scraps of shiny paper and string into pom-poms. Then we made up a simple cheer.

It was so simple that even the youngest recruits could recite it. We practiced until my ears ached, and we could shout the cheer more-or-less together while shaking our pom-poms.

That afternoon April's garage was just
as noisy. After reading my note about the
Mouselympics, the children became as excited
as the mouseletes and the Critter Post recruits.

All the kids squeaked at once.

"Let's make miniature sports equipment!"

"We can use pipe cleaners or maybe Popsicle sticks for hurdles!"

"I'll make a balance beam!"

"We can use pot holders for gym mats."

Jill told Grayson, Nilla, and me, "You mice can keep one set of equipment for your games. We can sell all the others at the fair as 'dollhouse playground equipment.'"

Wyatt and Andy built a basketball court. Grayson, Nilla, and I had fun testing the hoops.

While we were catching our breath, I asked the kids if they knew about Arthur Kingston. Then I told them what we overheard in the post office.

Javier said, "I'll look him up in my art books!"

The next day, Mrs. Olson handed out a flyer about Mr. Kingston and the auction. She couldn't understand why the children already seemed to know about the artist.

Later, in April's garage, Tanya did her Mrs. Olson imitation again. "I had no idea Kingston was so well-known among young people. Even *I* didn't know he'd spent part of his youth in Crittertown."

Tanya laughed. Then she added in her own voice, "You should've seen her face when Javier started rattling off facts about Kingston's career." In Mrs. Olson's voice she added, "Why don't you write a report to be part of the auction exhibit?"

Javier groaned. "Just what I need—another homework assignment when I'd rather be drawing!"

"I can help you," April whispered.

Javier smiled. "That'd be great!"

When the children took a break from their crafts, April asked Javier to repeat what he'd learned about Arthur Kingston. Then she arranged it in paragraphs.

Recalling the grammar lesson from our days at school, I made sure each sentence had a noun, a verb, and a sprinkle of punctuation. By the time the report was finished, we all felt rather proud of it.

Chapter 10 *Bull's-eye*

To our surprise and delight, this short report was printed in the local newspaper, along with the notice about the upcoming auction and fair. According to the paper, "Depending on his schedule, Mr. Kingston might attend."

When he read that, Javier whooped so loud that Buttercup nearly jumped out of his fur. Grayson, Nilla, and I laughed.

I told the loud dog, "Now you know how Dot feels!"

Nilla grumbled, "She deserves every bark!"

Javier gushed, "Wouldn't it be cool if I could meet Mr. Kingston and get his autograph and maybe even show him my sketchbook?"

Nilla tapped my shoulder. "What's an autograph?"

I shrugged and suggested, "Maybe we can stop by the library to ask Dictionaries."

I was eager for a chance to present Poetry with the cheese cracker.

As if reading my mind, Grayson asked, "What's in that box you've been carrying around?"

"Nothing," I fibbed. "It's just a box I made for Poetry. She…likes boxes. So I made one for her."

Grayson nodded. "Cheddar has a crush."

"What's a crush?" Nilla asked.

Grayson replied, "It's when a mouse who usually only cares about cheese suddenly starts thinking about Poetry."

We expected General History or at least some of his scouts to greet us outside the library. But we squeezed through the narrow passage into the basement before anyone noticed our arrival.

Grayson remarked, "No guards on duty?"

As before, Cookbooks' keen nose alerted the colony to our presence. "I smell…post office mice!" she said.

Travel rushed forward to embrace us. The tall mouse insisted on kissing us each first on one cheek and then on the other. She explained, "It's how they greet one another 'on the continent.'"

Nilla was puzzled. "On the condiment?"

"Continent," Grayson corrected. Then he

muttered, "But I still have no idea what she's talking about."

Cookbooks asked, "Are you here to see Nonfiction?"

I shrugged. "Nothing formal, just stopping by on our way home from making crafts with the children."

Nilla added, "Is Dictionaries around? I want to know what an autograph is, and maybe he can remind me about the difference between condiments and continents."

Grayson sighed. "One is stuff like ketchup and mustard, the other is a giant land mass."

"Oh," Nilla said. Then she bristled, "You'd think things that are wildly different wouldn't have names that sound so much alike!"

While they talked, my eyes scanned the crowded basement. Where was Poetry? I didn't want to have to ask for her—especially after Grayson's comment about my "crush."

Just as I was about to give up, someone tapped me on the shoulder. I turned around, and there she was!

I gave Poetry the box. While I'd measured the cracker and taped the cardboard sides, I'd made up all sorts of pretty speeches. Now that the moment had finally arrived, all I said was, "Here."

Poetry smiled. "Should I open it now?"

I saw Grayson and Nilla watching us.

"No!" I exclaimed. "No need. There's nothing in it, just a box, because I know you like them."

Poetry looked puzzled, but she played along. "Thank you. That's very thoughtful. It's the perfect size for…a box. Did you make it yourself?"

I blushed. "Thanks to all the crafts we've been doing lately, I've gotten pretty good with tape and scissors."

"So the crafts are coming along well?" Poetry asked.

Nilla jumped in. "You should see what the kids are making now! Mouse-sized sports equipment. It's awesome! We have our own basketball court!"

I added, "They're as excited about the Mouselympics as Grayson."

"Speaking of which," Grayson began, "Does your grandfather have a reply to my grandfather's letter?"

Poetry nodded. "We were going to send it by squirrel tomorrow morning."

Grayson said, "We can save Chitchat the trouble and take it when we leave."

I tried to tell from Poetry's face whether Nonfiction's response to the treaty was positive. But how could I know if that's why she was smiling, or if she was smiling at Grayson or—dare I hope—at me?

Grayson asked, "Is your brother still practicing metallurgy? Or is he too busy training for the Mouselympics?"

Before Poetry could reply, General History raced past us with three soldiers huffing and puffing behind him.

Poetry laughed. "There's your answer. If he isn't running, he's throwing javelins or practicing his high jump."

"What are javelins?" Nilla asked.

"A kind of spear," Dictionaries explained. "The javelin toss is an ancient Olympic event, dating from when the games were used as training for warriors."

Nilla declared, "I want to learn to throw javelins!"

General History ran backward until he

stopped in front of Nilla, panting. "Allow me to show you how."

Nilla glared at him. Then she turned her back without squeaking a word.

Poetry whispered, "What's the matter with her?"

"It's complicated," I replied.

I was pleased to see that General History didn't give up on Nilla. He said, "Haven't you heard the expression 'all's fair in love and war'?"

Nilla turned to glare at him again. "Don't you know I hate expressions?"

"But you'll love throwing javelins. You really must try it," General History went on. "Please let me escort you to the practice area."

Nilla's curiosity won out over her anger. She was soon tossing sharpened paper clips at a target. I heard her squeal happily, "Look! I almost hit the bull's-eye." Then she added,

"Why do they call the dot in the center the bull's-eye?"

History laughed and admitted, "I don't know! But if you keep practicing, you're sure to hit it. You're a natural!"

Nilla grinned.

General History handed her a bunch of javelins tied with string. "Take these back to the post office when you leave."

Nilla asked, "Why?"

General History explained, "I want the post office colony to have plenty of time to practice with these—so when the library colony wins we can say we beat you fair and square."

Nilla asked, "What do squares have to do with being fair?"

And we all laughed.

As our laughter was dying down, Nilla took careful aim at the target and flung a javelin with all her might. With a satisfying THUNK, it landed right in the center. Nilla giggled. "What makes you think the library colony will win?"

After enduring two more kisses from Travel, we departed, climbing onto Buttercup's neck, carrying the javelins and Nonfiction's letter.

Grayson said, "Looks like he wrote a letter as long as the one Pops sent. Why would they need so many words just to arrange for the Mouselympics?"

Not wanting to give away the secret, I shrugged. If all went well, Nonfiction's letter would say he agreed to the treaty. And he might have some ideas for changes.

If not… I didn't want to think about war.

The fact that General History was so excited about the Mouselympics was certainly cause for happy thoughts.

As we scrambled off Buttercup's neck, Grayson observed, "What's going on, Cheddar? You seem as twitchy as Twitchy!"

I took a deep breath and tried to sound casual. "Really? I'm fine. Maybe just a little tired from having the recruits squeaking in my ears all morning."

Still, I couldn't help trotting as I carried the scroll to Brownback's nest. Grayson's grandfather was also eager to discover Nonfiction's response.

He ripped at the ribbon tied around the library leader's letter. When he unrolled it, I recognized my own paw-writing.

For one horrible moment, I thought Nonfiction had returned the truce because he was rejecting it. Then I saw his signature at the bottom. In large, elegant script he had written "Nonfiction, Leader of the Library Clan."

I pointed to it and told Nilla, "*That* is an autograph!"

Brownback smiled and shouted, "Bring me a pen! Let's make this official."

Grayson asked, "What do you need a pen for, Pops?"

"Just bring it!" his grandfather yelled in a rare fit of impatience.

As soon as Grayson returned with the pen, Brownback signed his name next to Nonfiction's. "There, now there will be peace," he told Grayson.

When his grandson still looked puzzled, Brownback added, "From now on the only fighting between the post office and library clans will be in fair games during the Mouselympics."

Grayson finally understood. "So your 'letter' was a truce."

Brownback patted him on the back. "Exactly! Much better than a war; we're forming the first United Mouse Colonies."

I smiled. "That's as good as melted mozzarella!"

The third graders dug through their toy boxes and "mouseable" scraps to create more clever events for the Mouselympics. Wyatt turned an old mini car racetrack into a running track with Popsicle stick hurdles. April used an empty onion bag to make a volleyball net.

Grayson, Nilla, and I had a wonderful time learning all these sports and then teaching them to the library colony's mouselets. Like General History with the javelins, we made sure that the library mice had the same equipment as our team to practice for the big event. That way, the post office mouseletes could "win fair and square."

Since the children were so busy preparing for the crafts fair, we scheduled the Mouselympics for the weekend after that. I hoped we'd also be celebrating the rescue of Crittertown Elementary School. If not, we'd at least have an exciting event to take our minds off our troubles.

As the day of the fair drew near, everyone in town got into the spirit. Many summer people, whose mail was usually forwarded until well after the first crocus, came back to town early. They wanted a chance to meet *the* Arthur Kingston and to support Crittertown Elementary School.

Newspapers and radio shows kept talking up the event. The Crittertown B&B provided muffins and coffee. The bakery donated cookies. And to my extreme delight, the Crittertown Market provided its finest cheese platter.

It took every ounce of my strength not to go near that platter while all the humans were milling around admiring Mr. Kingston's early work. Just in case I felt too tempted, Nilla kept a tight grip on my tail.

Javier examined the sketches and grinned. "Look! He wasn't 'great' yet. His work wasn't even much better than mine," he told April.

She whispered, "I think your drawings are better than these."

Luckily, the citizens of Crittertown thought that even the early doodles of a famous artist were worth lots of money. As they bid for each picture, Nilla tried to make sense of the numbers on the blackboard.

She said, "I can't do subtraction in my head. Are they close to having enough money to fix the school?"

I smiled. "Very close."

Then all the humans suddenly started murmuring. "He's here!" "It's Mr. Kingston!" "The artist is here!"

We stared at the little old man with the wispy white hair poking out of a battered hat. Mr. Kingston smiled at everyone. He shook a few paws and nodded at some kind words. Then he went over to the crafts table.

The artist pronounced the Mouselympics equipment "quite clever." When he saw April's collection of "imagination doors," his wrinkled face lit with a delighted smile. "Oh! I must have all of these. They will make great gifts for my students."

Mr. Kingston insisted on paying "an outrageous" amount of money for the doors. ("Outrageous" according to the thrifty humans gossiping nearby. I thought it was just right.)

When the school secretary finished the math, I thought she might faint. "It's more than enough," she said. "The school is saved!"

Everyone cheered.

We'd barely recovered from the excitement of the fair when it was time for the

Mouselympics. We didn't have a torch to carry through the streets like they do at the start of the human Olympics. So the children made a paw print flag that led the parade from the library to the post office and finally to April's garage. Buttercup barked all the way.

The children took turns pulling the wagon full of mouseletes and those of us from both colonies who wanted to watch the games. If any grown-up came near, the children quickly covered us mice with stuffed animals. So it looked like the parade was "just for toys."

The Mouselympics equipment was all set up in April's garage. The girls had made tiny medals out of candy wrappers: gold foil for first prize and silver for second. Andy and Wyatt arranged building blocks to form a podium, so the winners of each event could stand there proudly to receive their medals.

Brownback and Nonfiction announced the opening of the games. They also briefly described the treaty joining our two clans.

"What's all the squeaking about?" Tanya wondered.

I wrote, "The treaty."

Bill groaned. "You know how politicians love to make speeches."

Perhaps the two leaders could tell the rest of the crowd felt the same way, because they quickly ended their remarks. Brownback said, "And now for the first event."

Nonfiction added, "The paw race."

The runners lined up at the starting line. Andy lifted a trumpet to his lips. Wyatt said,

"On your mark, get set…" Andy blew the horn

just as Wyatt said, "Go!"

I hadn't expected to get so caught up in the excitement. After all, it was just a race. But as Grayson and General History pulled out in front of the other mouseletes, I leaped to my feet with a pounding heart.

Charlie nudged me. "Shouldn't we cheer?"

I'd almost forgotten the pom-poms gripped in my paws. For a moment, I couldn't remember one word of the cheer we'd practiced over and over. Then the recruits' high squeaks filled my ears and I joined in:

"Who's the team with the most? Yaaaaay.... post! Give me a 'P'; give me an 'O.' Yaaaaay.... P.O.!"

I can't claim that our cheer really made a difference. But it seemed like our squeaks gave Grayson the boost he needed.

As he and General History crossed the finish line, the whole crowd held its breath. Wyatt sounded like a real sportscaster when he announced, "Grayson of Team Post Office wins by a whisker!"

At first General History looked angry. Then he smiled and shook Grayson's paw. "Good race," he said loudly. In a whisper he added, "I'll beat you next year!"

Grayson laughed. "Maybe you will—and maybe you won't!"

The library clan won the volleyball and basketball games. Grayson shook his head. "I told you we needed more team practice!"

Our clan took home the gold for pencil vaulting and the long jump. Grayson's chest puffed with pride to display his three gold medals. There would be no end to his bragging now! But it was nice to see my friend so happy.

Charlie tugged my fur. "Don't you want a gold medal?"

I touched the paw print necktie given to me as the Postmouseter. I said, "This is all the prize I need."

Charlie's skinny friend snickered. "Cheddar won't get a gold medal until they add a cheese-eating contest."

I decided to ignore him, although I couldn't help imagining the "Cheeselympics": a mozzarella pull, a slicing contest, a grating relay, a nibbling race...

Charlie squeezed my paw and pulled me out of my cheesy dream. "It's Nilla's event, the javelin toss!"

After the first round of throws, the contest came down to Nilla and General History. She looked so small standing next to him. My breakfast started jumping in my belly all over again.

Nilla had been practicing every day since General History gave us those sharpened paper clips. I'd seen her hit the bull's-eye many times. But would she win today? No one could know! Now I understood why humans made such a fuss about sports.

Nilla's paws shook. I hadn't seen her this nervous since that horrible day we visited the Crittertown Market.

Her first toss hit the target, but nowhere near the bull's-eye. Nilla bowed her head in shame.

The library mice cheered as General History prepared to toss his paper clip. Charlie nudged me again and whispered, "They don't have pom-poms or a rhyme."

General History wiped his eyes and then tossed his javelin. Had the cheer distracted him? Or was he just tired from the other events? For whatever reason, his paper clip was no closer to the bull's-eye than Nilla's.

The garage grew quiet before their second throw. Charlie opened his mouth, but I shook my head and whispered, "Let's save our cheers until after the toss."

Nilla flung her javelin. It sailed through the air and hit the center with a solid THUNK!

I leaped to my feet and cheered. The recruits shook their pom-poms and squeaked at the top of their little lungs. So did the rest of the post office clan. The third graders cheered, "Go Nilla!"

Once again, the garage fell silent. General History looked grim and very determined as he picked up his second javelin. He drew back his paw and tossed the sharpened paper clip. Every muscle of his body rippled with the effort. Even his toes clenched.

The paper clip flew through the air toward the target. It pierced the bull's-eye with a loud THUNK! The library clan cheered.

Charlie emitted a low "boo" until I put my paw on his shoulder and whispered, "Only cheers."

He understood. "Only happy thoughts."

I nodded and then took a deep breath. Nilla

looked scared. I knew how much she wanted to win.

Charlie squeezed my paw. His little eyes shone, and he held his breath. I held mine, too!

Nilla flung back her paw and tossed her third javelin. As she completed the throw, one of her feet slipped. I knew even before it hit the target that she hadn't made the bull's-eye.

Charlie slumped. Nilla paced. Maybe General History would miss on his third toss, too. I crossed my fingers the way I'd seen the humans do when they were worried and hoping for good luck.

General History's eyes narrowed. His focus was so intense that we all felt it. He threw the paper clip with easy grace. It flew like a bird to its nest. This javelin was going home. The only sound in the garage was the THUNK as the tip struck exactly in the center of the bull's-eye.

The library clan cheered with excitement! Charlie sighed. I uncrossed my fingers. Nilla wiped a tear from one eye before taking her place on the silver medalist's podium.

From the taller block, General History said, "Maybe you'll win the gold next year."

Nilla's smile returned. "You better keep practicing—or I just might!"

Since there were no cheese-eating or letter-writing contests, I didn't win any prizes. But I felt like a winner when Poetry found me during the post-games party.

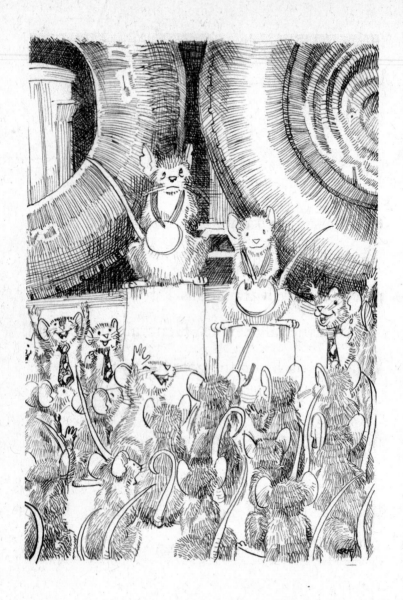

She said, "Thank you for the cheese cracker. It was very noble of you to give it to me. I know how much you love cheese."

I gazed into her big, beautiful eyes and wondered if she knew what I was thinking. Was it possible that I loved her even more than cheese itself?

So much had happened since the Change: understanding and making friends with small humans, saving the post office and the school, becoming the Postmouseter, helping to create a treaty between our clan and the library's. It seemed that anything was possible. Maybe even that Poetry might love me, too!